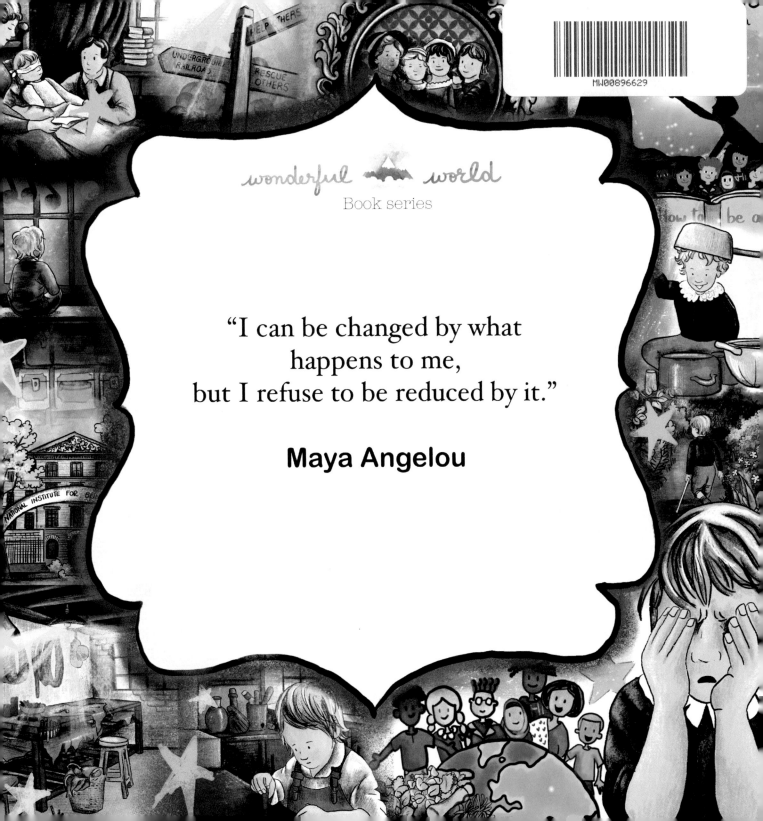

Book series

"I can be changed by what
happens to me,
but I refuse to be reduced by it."

Maya Angelou

Louis Braille

was a bright

and a **brilliant**
little boy,

Brilliant: Excellent; Could also mean
something that is shiny and bright.

Who loved to make music,
and play with his toys.

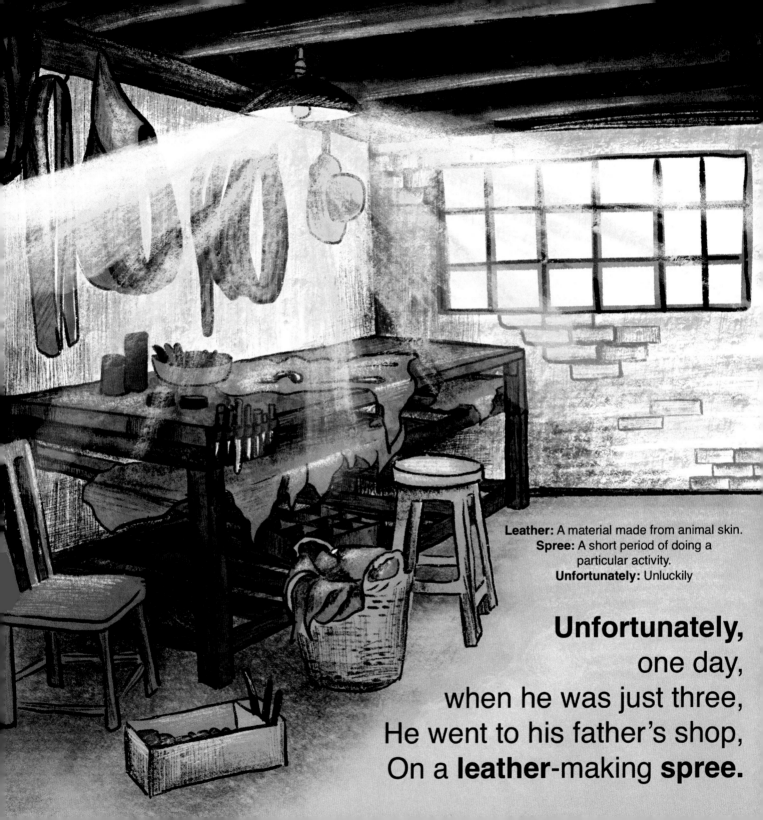

Leather: A material made from animal skin.
Spree: A short period of doing a particular activity.
Unfortunately: Unluckily

Unfortunately,
one day,
when he was just three,
He went to his father's shop,
On a **leather**-making **spree.**

Awl: A tool that looks like a long, sharp needle. It is used to poke holes in leather or wood.

And it was a bad idea,
Because when using the **awl,**
He poked his own eye,
And couldn't see at all.

They tried every **treatment,**
But it was all in vain.

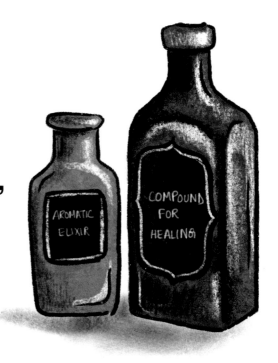

(Medical) Treatment: Special care given to make someone feel better.

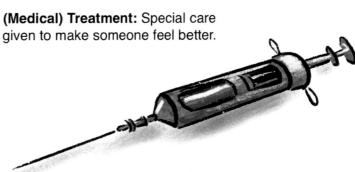

By the time he was five,
He'd totally lost his **sight.**
Louis couldn't understand
Why there was never any light.

Sight: What we see; Being able to see

But Louis and his parents,
Were so amazingly brave.
Instead of **lamenting** what they lost,
They **focused** on what they saved.

Focus: Paying attention to something.
Lament: To show sadness or disappointment.

His parents helped him study, and taught him many things,
So he could lead a full life, just like his three **siblings.**

Siblings: Children of the same parent or parents.

His father made for him
A special stick to swing,
So that when he walked,
He wouldn't bump into anything.

And Louis was very clever.
He really loved to learn.
He also wanted to teach,
And play music, and to earn.

So he had to move to Paris,
When he was only ten,
To attend a special school
Meant just for **blind** children.

Blind: People who are not able to see
have a condition called 'blindness'.
This can be in one eye or both.

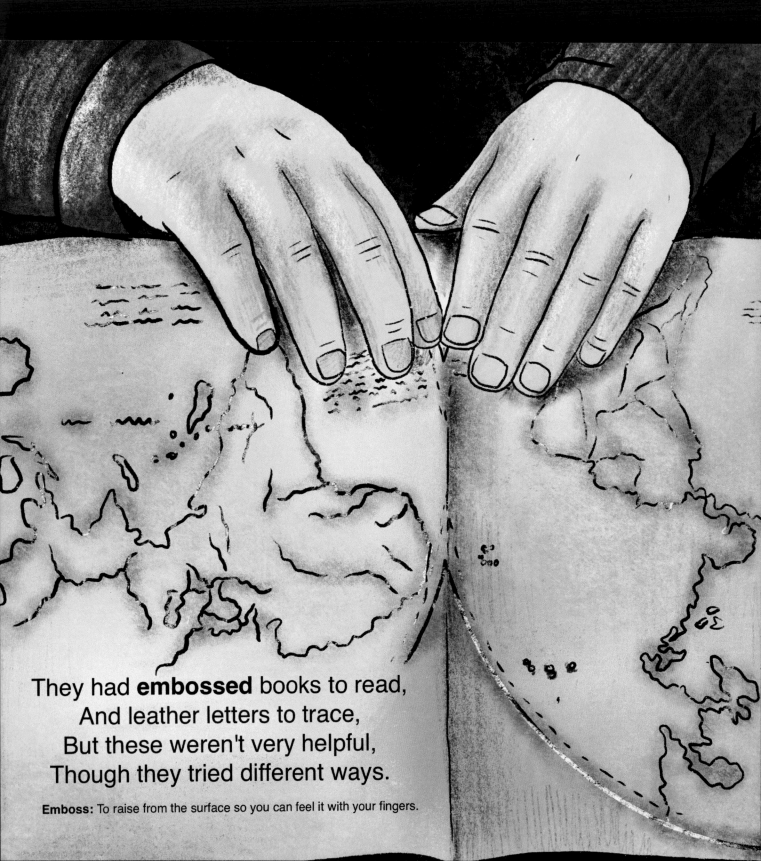

They had **embossed** books to read,
And leather letters to trace,
But these weren't very helpful,
Though they tried different ways.

Emboss: To raise from the surface so you can feel it with your fingers.

But Louis was determined,
That he'd never be pitied,
So he set about to find,
A different way to read.

He invented the braille system,
So that even without sight,
With the touch of their fingers,
The blind could read and write.

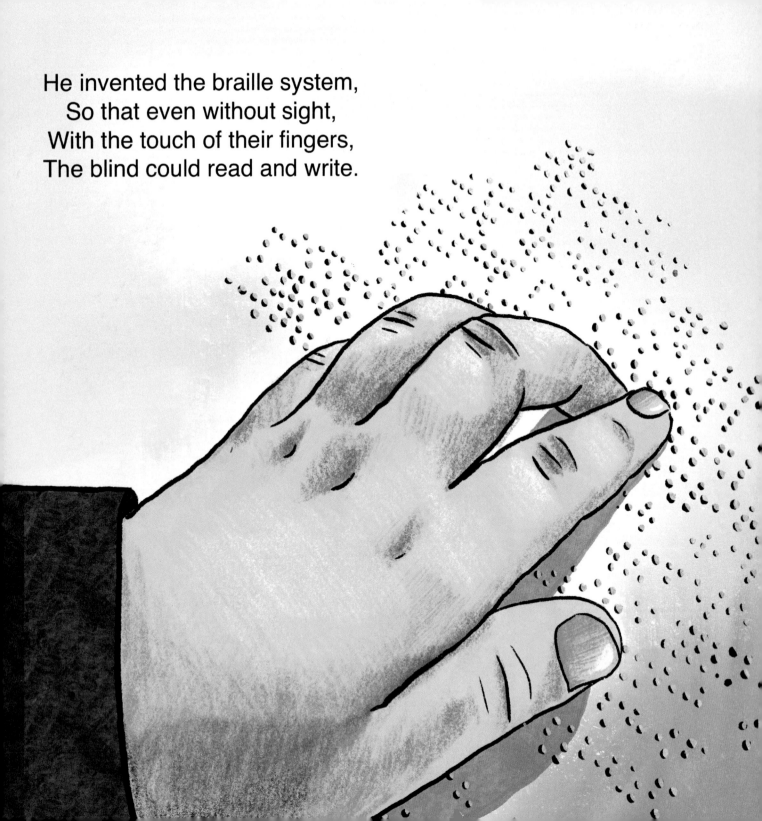

He used six embossed dots,
In different combinations
for letters and for numbers,
And even for punctuation!

Through his hard work
He became a musician,
And a **renowned** professor,
Who helped with education.

Renowned: Famous

You see, what kept him back,
Also made him strong,
And If you do your best like him,
You really can't go wrong.

Louis was brave and clever,
and very **tenacious** too,

Tenacious: Holding onto
something strongly.

He was a wonderful person,
Just like you!

wonderful world
Book series

"Storms make trees take
deeper roots."

Dolly Parton

wonderful world

Book series

The Beginning

Thanks for reading my book.
I hope you've enjoyed it. For an independent author, ratings
are very important for the success of their book. I'd be
grateful if you could take a minute to rate this book on
Amazon/ Goodreads.
Your support makes all the difference.

Glossary

Awl
A tool that looks like a long, sharp needle. It is used to poke holes in leather or wood.

Blind
People who are not able to see have a condition called 'blindness'. This can be in one eye or both.

Brilliant
Excellent; Could also mean something that is shiny and bright.

Emboss
To raise from the surface so you can feel it with your fingers.

Focus
Paying attention to something.

Lament
To show sadness or disappointment.

Leather
A material made from animal skin.

Glossary

Renowned
Famous

Siblings
Children of the same parent or parents.

Sight
What we see; Being able to see.

Spree
A short period of doing a particular activity.

Tenacious
Holding onto something strongly.

(Medical) Treatment
Special care given to make someone feel better.

Unfortunately
Unluckily

Write your name in braille

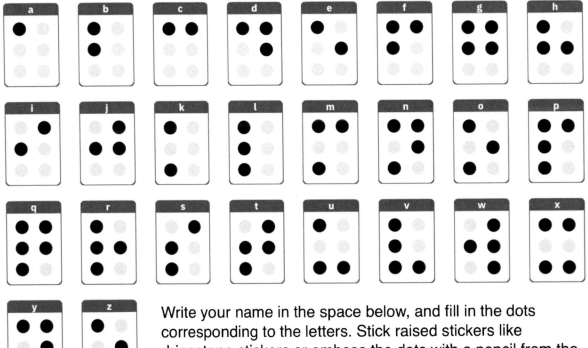

Write your name in the space below, and fill in the dots corresponding to the letters. Stick raised stickers like rhinestone stickers or emboss the dots with a pencil from the back of the sheet so you can use your finger to read braille.

Name _____

Cut Line
Fold Line

A simplified French cottage of the type Louis Braille lived in with his family in Coupvray.

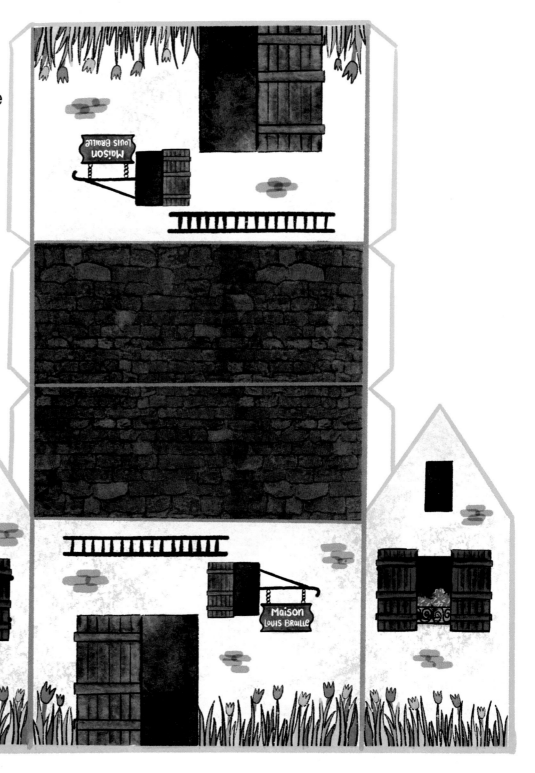

wonderful  *world*
Book series

About the Author

Author, illustrator, and dentist, **Ramya Julian** finished her first novel at the age of ten and she avers it was very well received though it was read only by her brother.

She has all the hobbies of a maiden Victorian aunt – reading, writing, painting, crocheting, knitting and sewing, and the temperament of one. When she's not guilt-tripping her two daughters into good behaviour, she can be found devouring books, crafting poems and puns, and chuckling at her own witticisms. She grew up in India and now lives with her husband and their two daughters in London.

She has experienced so much joy through the enchanting artistry of many authors and creators, that she aspires to share at least some of it through her writing.

To see more of her work, visit **www.ramyajulian.com**

LOUIS BRAILLE

Timeline

4th January 1809

The youngest of four siblings, Louis Braille was born in Coupvray, a small French town, to Simon-René and Monique.

1812

At the age of three, he stabbed himself in the eye while playing in his father's leather workshop, and lost his vision soon after.

1819

Because of his intelligence and hardwork, Braille was allowed to attend the Royal Institute for Blind Youth in February 1819.

1821

Braille learned about Charles Barbier's 'night writing' system, which used raised dots to represent sounds. This inspired him to develop his own system.

1837

The second edition discarded the dashes as smaller cells meant letters could be read by a single touch of a finger.

1829

Braille published the first version of his system titled 'Procedure for Writing Words, Music, and Plainsong in Dots'.

1824

At the age of 15, Braille invented the Braille system by using six-dot cells to represent letters and numbers. This allowed for a simpler way for the visually impaired to read and write.

1839

Braille further refined his system to include musical notations. He was an accomplished cellist and organist.

January 6th 1852

Louis Braille died at the age of 43 from tuberculosis, an illness he had lived with for 16 years.

1854

Two years after his death, the Braille system was officially adopted by the Royal Institute for Blind Youth, at the insistence of its pupils.

1932

A universal Braille code for English was adopted which was further refined in 1957.

HELLO

Thank you for reading my book!

What appealed to me the most about Louis Braille's story is that it shows how resilient the human spirit is. Imagine losing your vision at the age of five! I found his question 'Why is it always dark?' especially poignant. But the fact that he invented a way for those who are visually impaired to read as fast as those with sight is amazing. 300-400 words a minute, and all with the touch of a finger!
He came. He couldn't see. He invented.

I feel we often approach disability (any sort of 'divergence', actually) from a place of pity and condescension, which is well, a pity. Rather, I think our efforts would be more usefully employed if we worked to make the world more inclusive so everyone can navigate it with more ease and less fear.

For instance, if you saw a toy in a blind person's path, would you clear the toy, or grab their arm to guide them around it?
It starts with the little things, doesn't it?

I loved Braille's story of courage and creativity, of innovation and incredible strength.

If humanity produces people such as this,
there is hope for us, don't you agree?

Love,
Ramya

Check out
www.ramyajulian.com/picturebooks

www.ramyajulian.com

Also in this series

NEXT IN LINE: MANY MANY MORE
WONDERFUL DIVERSE HEROES

TO MY NEWSLETTER
For the latest news and
free printables
www.ramyajulian.com

@RAMYAJULIAN

wonderful world

Book series

Journals

FILLED WITH QUOTES FROM FAMOUS CLASSIC NOVELS

Funny Factory PRODUCTIONS™

The perfect gift for book lovers

Available on Amazon

15597102R00021